W9-ARK-960

for
Janek
&
Franek

My Four Seasons

Illustrated by Dawid Ryski

LITTLE
GESTALTEN

Here we are. This is my whole family on the first day of a new year.
Last but not least is Polly, our little dog.

During the night, just as the old year ends and the new one begins, it starts to snow. The whole city is sprinkled with frosty white powder. As we stamp through the crunchy, cushiony carpet, making deep tracks, we enjoy the sound our steps make in the quiet city.

The snow stays for a long, long time. But after lots of slipping, sliding, sledding, and skiing, patches of old grass shine through. Curly crocuses and white snowdrops with spots of green begin to poke out from the frozen earth. We make the most of one last slide before the early evening sets in.

Suddenly, the sun is warmer. The snow has all melted away and we can leave our scarves and gloves at home. Spring has sprung! Succulent seedlings appear all over the place and the smells of pink cherry blossoms and apple trees drift through the air. The honeybees buzz busily around, collecting nectar.

The garden is green and at last we can plant out our flowers and vegetables. Our little lettuces, petite potatoes, and minuscule marrows will grow big. Around us, the birds twitter happily and Polly yaps playfully. The whistling wind doesn't make us shiver anymore.

Once the sun and wind have dried up the last of the spring puddles,
it's time to start playing our summer games. We can wear shorts again!
The whole park is full of gregarious giggles and spritely shrieks.
At school, though, we stare out the windows, waiting to go outside.
The time drags by like a lazy snail.

At long last, school is out. It's the middle of summer! We wake up with the sunshine streaming into our rooms and go to bed while the sun is still out. Running around all day long, exploring every little bit of our world, we lark about, taste fried fish, frosty lemonade, and take little licks of ice cream. After our evening barbecue, we toast marshmallows and see who can stay awake the longest.

On the weekend, we take a trip to the lake. Because we want to camp, we take our tent. For the entire day, we play in the water, swimming like frogs or paddling like dogs. We sail off in our rubber boat, pretending to be petulant pirates and savage sea beasts. Before we fall asleep, we spot the shapes of far off stars hanging in the dark skies.

But even the longest holidays come to an end. The grain in the fields is ripe and ready to harvest, and the sun goes down earlier in the evenings. It's time go back to school and kindergarten.

The leaves change to yellow, orange, and red, and the rain falls more often. In the forest hunting for mushrooms, we load our baskets with white, brown, and gray fungi. We play hide and seek in the multicolored woods, moving sneakily like furtive foxes and shuffling low to the ground like bristly hedgehogs.

It starts to rain more often, and one day the wind whips up a storm. Thick, dark clouds gather, the thunder claps, and the lightning flashes. Leaves scoot through the air and the world is topsy-turvy. After a while, the weather calms and we can fly our kites. They glide as we chase through long, soggy grass and spot squirrels scuttling about gathering their winter supplies.

Though it's getting chilly outside, we have something to look forward to: Halloween. We dress up as hideous monsters, frightful ghosts, and stupendously strong superheroes and go trick or treating. People give us candy as we walk from house to house. Back at home in the warmth, we tip out our bounty. Our cheeks shine as bright as the Halloween pumpkins.

One morning, we wake up and the first frost has arrived. Tiny speckles of white are falling and the ground looks crisp. Winter has begun. We rush out and slide across frozen puddles, breathing clouds of fog and waiting excitedly for the holidays to come.

1982
18

Finally, the holidays come around. Christmas is only a few days away and the snow is slowly building up outside. We go on vacation to the mountains and build the biggest snowman the world has ever seen. Then come the snowball fights. The one who is covered in the most snow loses.

In the evening, we all sit around the fire and tell each other tales. Polly the dog is there, too. Sometimes the stories are true and other times they are made-up—imagined from our adventures over the past seasons. We wonder what next year will bring, and make plans. There is a lot to think about because we are already one year older!

My Four Seasons

Illustrated by Dawid Ryski

This book was conceived, edited, and designed by Gestalten.

Concept by Hendrik Hellige
Texts by Amy Visram

Published by Little Gestalten, Berlin 2017

ISBN: 978-3-89955-784-8

The German edition is available under ISBN 978-3-89955-783-1.

Typefaces: Avenir by Adrian Frutiger, Neutraface by House Industries

Printed by Offsetdruckerei Grammlich, Pliezhausen
Made in Germany

For more information, please visit little.gestalten.com.

Bibliographic information published by the Deutsche Nationalbibliothek: The Deutsche Nationalbibliothek lists this publication in the Deutsche Nationalbibliografie; detailed bibliographic data are available online at http://dnb.d-nb.de.

This book was printed on paper certified according to the standards of the FSC®.